A Note to Parents and Caregivers:

Read-it! Readers are for children who are just starting on the amazing road to reading. These beautiful books support both the acquisition of reading skills and the love of books.

The PURPLE LEVEL presents basic topics and objects using high frequency words and simple language patterns.

The RED LEVEL presents familiar topics using common words and repeating sentence patterns.

The BLUE LEVEL presents new ideas using a larger vocabulary and varied sentence structure.

The YELLOW LEVEL presents more challenging ideas, a broad vocabulary, and wide variety in sentence structure.

The GREEN LEVEL presents more complex ideas, an extended vocabulary range, and expanded language structures.

The ORANGE LEVEL presents a wide range of ideas and concepts using challenging vocabulary and complex language structures.

When sharing a book with your child, read in short stretches, pausing often to talk about the pictures. Have your child turn the pages and point to the pictures and familiar words. And be sure to reread favorite stories or parts of stories.

There is no right or wrong way to share books with children. Find time to read with your child, and pass on the legacy of literacy.

Adria F. Klein, Ph.D.
Professor Emeritus
California State University
San Bernardino, California

Editor: Jill Kalz
Designer: Hilary Wacholz
Page Production: Melissa Kes
Art Director: Nathan Gassman
Associate Managing Editor: Christianne Jones
The illustrations in this book were created with watercolor and digitally.

Picture Window Books
151 Good Counsel Drive
P.O. Box 669
Mankato, MN 56002-0669
877-845-8392
www.picturewindowbooks.com

Printed in the United States of America.

All books published by Picture Window Books
are manufactured with paper containing at least
10 percent post-consumer waste.

Library of Congress Cataloging-in-Publication Data
Meister, Cari.
Robin Hood and the tricky butcher / retold by Cari Meister ; illustrated by
Necdet Yilmaz.
p. cm. — (Read-it! readers: legends)
ISBN 978-1-4048-4840-5 (library binding)
1. Robin Hood (Legendary character)—Legends. [1. Robin Hood (Legendary
character)—Legends. 2. Folklore—England.] I. Yilmaz, Necdet, 1970- ill. II. Title.
PZ8.1.M498Roe 2008
398.2—dc22   2008006319

Robin Hood
─and the─
Tricky Butcher

a retelling by Cari Meister
illustrated by Necdet Yilmaz

Special thanks to our reading adviser:

Adria F. Klein, Ph.D.
Professor Emeritus, California State University
San Bernardino, California

Long ago, a man named Robin Hood lived in Sherwood Forest. Robin Hood had a group of friends called the Merry Men.

Together, they saved people from danger.
They stole money from rich people and gave
it to the poor.

One day, Robin Hood and Little John met a stranger. The stranger had a pony and a full cart. He said he was a butcher.

"Where are you going?" asked Robin Hood.

"I'm going to the market," said the butcher.
"I have meat to sell."

Robin Hood had not been to town for a long time. He wanted to have some fun.

"I will give you four gold coins for your pony and cart," he told the butcher.

"Five gold coins," said the butcher.

"OK," said Robin Hood. "But give me your coat and hat, too."

"You can't go to town," said Little John. "The sheriff of Nottingham doesn't like you. He will throw you in jail!"

But Robin Hood had a plan. He put a patch over one eye. He put on the butcher's coat and hat. "The sheriff will never know it's me!" he said.

The market was busy. Some people sold bread and meat. Others sold eggs and honey.

"Come and buy!" Robin Hood called from his cart. "This is the best meat in the market!"

13

Robin Hood's prices were lower than anyone else's. Soon the meat would be gone.

"He must be a fool!" said the other butchers. "No one sells meat so cheap!"

The sheriff was in the market that day. He watched the strange butcher.

"Perhaps this fool has more meat to sell," the sheriff thought. "I will buy it for a little gold. Then I will sell it for a lot of gold!"

The sheriff loved gold more than anything else.

"Butcher," said the sheriff, "please come to my house for dinner."

The sheriff's wife served Robin Hood a tasty meal. He ate soup. He ate turkey. He ate potatoes, bread, and fruit.

"Thank you very much for the good food," Robin Hood said.

"I hope you will have dinner with us again," said the sheriff.

Robin Hood laughed. He had fooled the sheriff!

"Butcher, do you have more meat to sell?" the sheriff asked.

"I have two hundred fat deer," said Robin Hood. "Would you like to see them tomorrow morning?"

The sheriff nodded. He smiled an evil smile and went to bed.

That night, the sheriff dreamed of fat deer.
He dreamed of piles of gold.

The next morning, the sheriff tied three bags of gold to his saddle.

"How far are we going?" he asked Robin Hood.

"Not far," said Robin Hood.

Soon they came to Sherwood Forest.
Deer moved all around.

25

"Do you like my deer?" asked Robin Hood.

The deer in Sherwood Forest didn't belong to Robin Hood. They belonged to the king. Robin Hood knew that. The sheriff knew that, too.

"This is a trick!" said the sheriff. "Those aren't your deer. I'm leaving!"

Robin Hood blew his horn. The Merry Men came out from behind the trees.

"Look who came for a visit!" said Robin Hood.

The sheriff turned red. Now he knew it was Robin Hood in the blue coat.

Robin Hood untied the bags of gold from the sheriff's saddle.

"Thank you, sir!" he said. "Come back soon!"

The sheriff rode back to town, feeling very, very foolish. And Robin Hood rode off to give the gold to the poor.

More *Read-it!* Readers

Bright pictures and fun stories help you practice your reading skills. Look for more books at your level.

How Spirit Dog Made the Milky Way:
  A Retelling of a Cherokee Legend
King Arthur and the Black Knight
King Arthur and the Sword in the Stone
Mato the Bear and Devil's Tower:
  A Retelling of a Lakota Legend
Robin Hood and the Golden Arrow
Robin Hood and the Tricky Butcher

On the Web

FactHound offers a safe, fun way to find Web sites related to topics in this book. All of the sites on FactHound have been researched by our staff.

1. Visit *www.facthound.com*

2. Type in this special code:
   1404848401

3. Click on the FETCH IT button.

Your trusty FactHound will fetch the best sites for you!
A complete list of *Read-it!* Readers is available on our Web site:
www.picturewindowbooks.com